I SPY
SPECTACULAR

A BOOK OF PICTURE RIDDLES

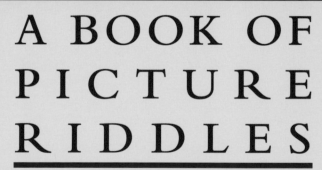

Photographs by Walter Wick

Riddles by Jean Marzollo

Cartwheel
B·O·O·K·S·®

SCHOLASTIC INC.
New York   Toronto   London   Auckland
Sydney   Mexico City   New Delhi   Hong Kong

For Gabriel Claudio Marzollo, with thanks
to Papa Dave and Uncle Dan

J.M.

For my spectacular wife, Linda

W.W.

Text compilation copyright © 2011 by Jean Marzollo.
Photo compilation copyright © 2011 by Walter Wick.

Cover illustration "Sorting and Classifying" from *I Spy School Days* copyright
© 1995 by Walter Wick. "Blocks" and "Round & Round" from *I Spy* © 1992 by Walter Wick;
"Arrival" and "View from Duck Pond Inn" from *I Spy Treasure Hunt* © 1999 by Walter Wick;
"Window Shopping" and "Nutcracker Sweets" from *I Spy Christmas* © 1992 by Walter Wick;
"On the Boardwalk," "Carnival Warehouse," and "Fun House Mirror" from *I Spy Fun House*
© 1993 by Walter Wick; "The Golden Cage" and "The Naughty Kittens" from *I Spy Mystery*
© 1993 by Walter Wick; "Ballerina" from *I Spy Fantasy* © 1994 by Walter Wick.
All published by Scholastic Inc.

Library of Congress Cataloging-in-Publication is available.

ISBN 978-0-545-22278-5
10 9 8 7 6 5 4 3 2 1   11 12 13 14 15 16
Printed in China   62 • First printing, April 2011

TABLE OF CONTENTS

Picture riddles fill this book;
Turn the pages! Take a look!

Use your mind, use your eye;
Read the riddles — play I SPY!

I spy a beard, two knots that are tied,
Two propellers, a ladder, and a ladle slide;

Five holes for eyes, a Y, a two,
Four yellow tines, and two hats of blue.

9

I spy a crow, a green-and-yellow eye,

Four backpacks, a man's red tie;

A nine, a knife, a HOUSE FOR SALE,
A spring, a bug, and a place to send mail.

I spy a football, BRITAIN, PERU,
A tambourine, wings of blue;

An apron, two clowns, a lion's tail,
A domino, and a wedding veil.

I spy a dragon, a small silver ear,

1978, a bottle cap, a gear;

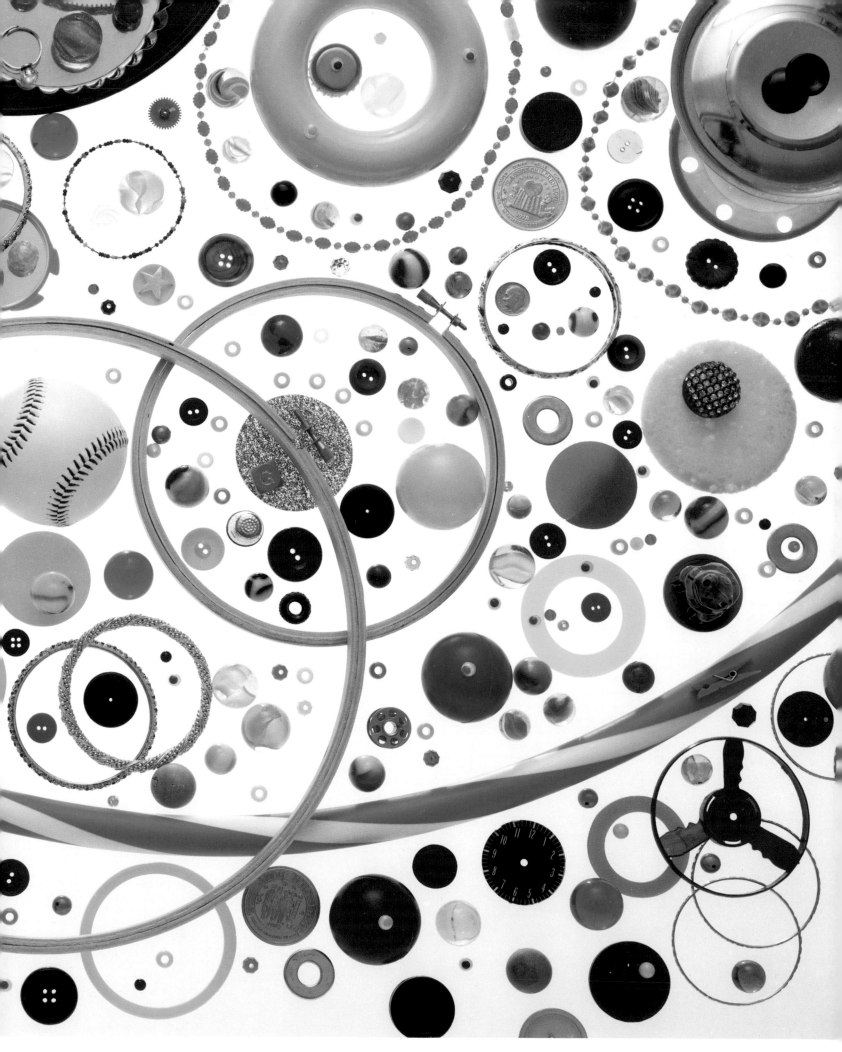

Two five-hole buttons, a red rubber band,
Four washers, and oceans surrounding land.

I spy a shovel, a bottle, a bee,

A nail, a donkey, a wooden tee;

A length of hose, a fox, a snail,
A sneaky black cat, and a small red pail.

I spy a trophy, a hammering tool,
A small paper clip, a swan, a stool;

Two springs, a trunk, a little white hat,
A camera, a comb, a key, and a bat.

I spy a fish, a jack, a Q,

A tambourine, and socks that are blue;

A horse with a rider, a moon, a three,
Four bunny ears, and a little green tee.

I spy a cup for tea, a crown,

A top hat, a dog, PLUMS, a frown;

A small blue flower, a teapot handle,
Three "pigtails," and a flame on a candle.

I spy two tickets, an upside-down A,
Seven clown buttons, a button that's gray;

Two gold wands, eight lizard feet,
An H, and an upside-down bicycle seat.

I spy a snowflake, a crown pin, a star,

An exclamation point, a small guitar;

A safety pin, a clasp, a sewing machine,
And a gold bobby pin clipped onto green.

I spy a shovel, a thimble, TOYS,

A sword, a cannon, two fast boys;

An eraser, two screws, two tires to fix,
Two ladders, and 1956.

EXTRA CREDIT RIDDLES

Find the Pictures That Go With These Riddles:

I spy a thimble, a yo-yo, too,

And two pairs of eyes looking at you.

I spy two pointing hands, a gear,

A sword for a nose, and an engineer.

I spy an umbrella, NUTCRACKER SUITE,

A black mustache, and dancing feet.

I spy a golf ball, GAME, a bat,

A giraffe's long neck, and a black top hat.

I spy a "no right turn" sign, a ticket,

And a man with a camera who's ready to click it.

I spy a lamb, the shadow of a sword,

Sand, and a mixer where cement is poured.

I spy a domino, a ring that's fine,

A rolling pin, and a broken line.

I spy a dog, a birdhouse, CARE,

A tiger, a deer, and an empty chair.

I spy a whistle, a fish, a red fan,

An umbrella, a shovel, and a small policeman.

I spy two scoops, two spools of thread,

And a polka-dot patch that's white and red.

I spy a candy cane, PURE, a chair,

A violin, and a bow-tie bear.

I spy a snowman, a lollipop heart,

A chocolate shell, and a shell smashed apart.

About the Creators of I Spy

JEAN MARZOLLO with **Dan Marzollo** and **Dave Marzollo**

Jean Marzollo has written over 130 books, including *Pierre the Penguin*; *Soccer Sam*; *Happy Birthday, Martin Luther King*; *The Little Plant Doctor*; *In 1776*; *Mama Mama / Papa Papa*; and *I Am a Caterpillar*, as well as books for parents and teachers, such as *Fathers and Babies* and *The New Kindergarten*. In recent years she has illustrated free interactive e-books for kids on her website: www.jeanmarzollo.com.

As a child, Jean loved to read and make things, especially dolls' clothes. She grew up in Manchester, Connecticut, and graduated from the University of Connecticut and Harvard Graduate School of Education. She lives with her husband in the Hudson River Valley, where her sons, Dan and Dave, grew up. As teenagers, her sons tested the first I Spy books, and now they help Jean write new I Spy books with original riddles based on the thousands of objects found in the eight classic I Spy books. They find interesting new objects to call for creatively within the traditional I Spy rhythm and rhyme pattern. "We try to avoid calling for the same thing twice," says Dan. "If we have to call for it again, we describe it in a different way," explains Dave. "That way we can keep the I Spy game as fresh and fun as the first I Spy book was twenty years ago."

WALTER WICK

Walter Wick is the award-winning photographer of the I Spy series as well as the author and photographer of the bestselling Can You See What I See? series. Walter has loved to tinker and invent ever since he was a child. After graduating from Paier College of Art, he soon developed a reputation as an ingenious photographic illustrator. In addition to illustrating posters for *Let's Find Out* and covers for *Newsweek*, *Psychology Today*, and *Discover*, Walter invented numerous photographic puzzles for *GAMES* magazine. After creating the photographic puzzles for the first I Spy book in 1991, Walter found the perfect audience for his unique vision. He has been creating acclaimed children's books ever since. His other books include *A Drop of Water: A Book of Science and Wonder*, which won numerous awards, including the Boston Globe/Horn Book Award for Nonfiction. His book *Walter Wick's Optical Tricks* was named a Best Illustrated Children's Book by the *New York Times Book Review* and a Notable Children's Book by the American Library Association, in addition to many other awards. Walter lives in Connecticut with his wife, Linda. More information about Walter Wick is available at www.walterwick.com and www.scholastic.com/canyouseewhatisee/.

CAROL DEVINE CARSON, the book designer for the first I Spy books, is art director at Alfred A. Knopf Publishers. She has designed covers for books by John Updike, Joan Didion, Alice Munro, Bill Clinton, and Pope John Paul II.

The Story of the First I Spy Book, *I Spy: A Book of Picture Riddles*

CELEBRATE **20** YEARS!

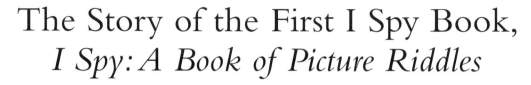

In 1986 award-winning children's book author Jean Marzollo was the editor of *Let's Find Out,* Scholastic's kindergarten magazine, working with Carol Devine Carson, a well-known art director. One day Jean and Carol received in the mail a fascinating promotional photograph of hardware-store-type objects from an amazing artist and photographer, Walter Wick. The minute Jean saw the photograph, she knew Walter's work would be perfect for kindergarten because the objects were so clearly and attractively presented. Carol and Jean asked Walter to make a classroom poster called "Fasteners," featuring zippers, buttons, paper clips, and so on. The result, published in January 1987, was gorgeous and well appreciated by kids and teachers. Jean and Carol asked Walter to create more wonderful pictures for *Let's Find Out.* Soon, Grace Maccarone and Bernette Ford of Scholastic's Cartwheel Books asked Jean to see if Carol and Walter were interested in making a children's book. They were.

Jean, Carol, and Walter worked together to create the first I Spy book for Scholastic. As they worked, they made sure that every beautiful I Spy photograph was educationally appropriate for young children, that every riddle was rich with vocabulary set in a pattern of rhythm and rhyme, and that the book was designed to invite children to sit up and start hunting.

I Spy: A Book of Picture Riddles was scheduled to be published in 1992, but key people at Scholastic became so excited about advance copies of the book that they rushed it into bookstores in the fall of 1991. While Jean, Carol, and Walter expected that young children would like I Spy, they were thrilled to discover that older kids and grown-ups liked it, too. No matter how cleverly Walter had hidden an object, he also had made certain that readers could find it eventually and that when they did, they would feel like heroes. Parents were amazed (and proud) to find that their children were sometimes better at I Spy than they were.

ACKNOWLEDGMENTS

We would like to thank all the people at Scholastic who have helped to publish the I Spy books through the years. We are especially grateful to our editors, Bernette Ford, Grace Maccarone, and Ken Geist. Special thanks to Molly Friedrich of The Friedrich Agency. Last but not least, we want to thank nine-year-old Stefan N. Linson, who did the final check of this book to make sure that everything could be found.

Happy Birthday and Happy Hunting!

Jean Marzollo and Walter Wick

"Kids find I Spy engaging because it builds on their excellent visual discrimination skills. It also challenges them incrementally with some initial success virtually guaranteed. Good teachers provide instruction this way — and it works! Another appeal of I Spy, besides the sheer beauty of Walter Wick's photographs, is their uniqueness. They capture our attention because they are different and interesting. Brain research tells us that learners respond to novelty. As children respond to I Spy, they improve their reading, writing, rhyming, critical thinking, and vocabulary skills."

—Dr. Joanne Marien, Superintendent, Somers Public Schools, Somers, NY